Cam's Kite

by Jackie Walter and Tomislav Zlatic

W
FRANKLIN WATTS
LONDON•SYDNEY

Cam had a new kite.

He went to the field
with Dad.

He took his kite.

The kite went up in the wind.

It went up and up and up.

"Oh no!" said Cam.

"My kite is in the tree."

Cam pulled and pulled.

8

But the kite was stuck.

Dad pulled and pulled.

But the kite was stuck.

"I can help!" said Dad.

Dad went up the tree.

Dad got the kite.

"Here you are," he said.

The kite went up in the wind.

It went up and up
and up and up.

"Oh no," said Dad.

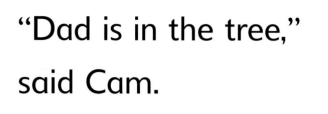

"Dad is in the tree,"
said Cam.

Story trail

Start at the beginning of the story trail. Ask your child to retell the story in their own words, pointing to each picture in turn to recall the sequence of events.

Start

Independent Reading

This series is designed to provide an opportunity for your child to read on their own. These notes are written for you to help your child choose a book and to read it independently.

In school, your child's teacher will often be using reading books which have been banded to support the process of learning to read.

Use the book band colour your child is reading in school to help you make a good choice. *Cam's Kite* is a good choice for children reading at Yellow Band in their classroom to read independently.

The aim of independent reading is to read this book with ease, so that your child enjoys the story and relates it to their own experiences.

About the book

Cam takes his new kite out to the field with Dad. The kite flies brilliantly, until it gets stuck in a tree. Cam cannot get it down, but Dad goes to the rescue.

Before reading

Help your child to learn how to make good choices by asking: "Why did you choose this book? Why do you think you will enjoy it?" Look at the cover together and ask: "What do you think the story will be about?" Support your child to think of what they already know about the story context. Read the title aloud and ask: "Do you think Cam might have a problem when he flies his kite? Why do you think that?" Remind your child that they can try to sound out the letters to make a word if they get stuck.

Decide together whether your child will read the story independently or read it aloud to you. When books are short, as at Yellow Band, your child may wish to do both!

During reading

If reading aloud, support your child if they hesitate or ask for help by telling the word. Remind your child of what they know and what they can do independently.

If reading to themselves, remind your child that they can come and ask for your help if stuck.

After reading

Support comprehension by asking your child to tell you about the story. Use the story trail to encourage your child to retell the story in the right sequence, in their own words.

Help your child think about the messages in the book that go beyond the story and ask: "Do you think Mum and Cam might have to help Dad get down from the tree? Why / why not?" Give your child a chance to respond to the story: "Did you have a favourite part? Have you ever flown a kite? Did it get stuck anywhere?"

Extending learning

Help your child understand the story structure by using the same sentence patterns and adding some new elements. "Let's make up a new story about Cam and his dad going to fly the kite. 'Oh no! My kite is in the pond,' said Cam. 'I can help!' said Dad. Dad got in the pond. He got the kite. 'Oh no!' said Dad. Now you try. Where will Cam's kite get stuck in your story?"

Your child's teacher will be talking about punctuation at Yellow Band. On a few of the pages, check your child can recognise capital letters, exclamation marks and full stops by asking them to point these out.

Franklin Watts
First published in Great Britain in 2019
by The Watts Publishing Group

Copyright © The Watts Publishing Group 2019

Series Editors: Jackie Hamley and Melanie Palmer
Series Advisors: Dr Sue Bodman and Glen Franklin
Series Designer: Peter Scoulding

A CIP catalogue record for this book is
available from the British Library.

ISBN 978 1 4451 6783 1 (hbk)
ISBN 978 1 4451 6785 5 (pbk)
ISBN 978 1 4451 6784 8 (library ebook)

Printed in China

Franklin Watts
An imprint of
Hachette Children's Group
Part of The Watts Publishing Group
Carmelite House
50 Victoria Embankment
London EC4Y 0DZ

An Hachette UK Company
www.hachette.co.uk

www.franklinwatts.co.uk

FSC
www.fsc.org
MIX
Paper from
responsible sources
FSC® C104740